Rose Gold

and Friends

Yasmeen's Winter Fun

Rose Gold
and Friends

Yasmeen's Winter Fun
ALICE HEMMING

SCHOLASTIC

Published in the UK by Scholastic Children's Books, 2019
Euston House, 24 Eversholt Street, London, NW1 1DB, UK
A division of Scholastic Limited.

London – New York – Toronto – Sydney – Auckland
Mexico City – New Delhi – Hong Kong

Text © Alice Hemming, 2019
Cover characters and inside Illustrations by Kerry LaRue © Scholastic Ltd, 2019

The right of Alice Hemming to be identified as the author of this work has been
asserted by her under the Copyright, Designs and Patents Act 1988.

ISBN 978 1407 19670 1

Printed by CPI Group (UK) Ltd, Croydon, CR0 4YY
Papers used by Scholastic Children's Books are made
from wood grown in sustainable forests.

1 3 5 7 9 10 8 6 4 2

www.scholastic.co.uk

for Georgie

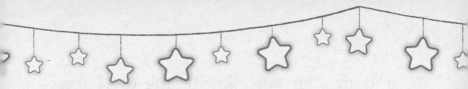

Chapter 1

Waiting For Ever

Yasmeen sat on a stool at the breakfast bar, bouncing her knee up and down rapidly. "Was that a car? I think I can hear someone outside!"

Her mum was busy unpacking groceries and sorting them into the kitchen cupboards. She stopped for a moment, holding a bunch of bananas in mid-air. "I'm sure they'll ring the buzzer when they get here. Just relax."

But Yasmeen couldn't. "Did you get all the food I asked for? Have we got tomato ketchup crisps? Oralie loves tomato ketchup flavoured crisps. And mini marshmallows? For hot chocolate?"

"I've got *everything* you put on the *very long* list," said Yasmeen's mum, holding out the scrap of paper. "Cakes, pizza, grapes, mini boxes of cereal... Nobody is going to go hungry this weekend." She paused. "But you must remember, Yasmeen, we're not expecting royalty. It's just your friends."

"Just my friends? *Just my friends?* You mean my *very best friends* in the *entire world*!"

Yasmeen had met the others – Amber, Rose and Oralie – at summer camp

and they had become friends instantly.
They had been planning this reunion
ever since. For once, her mum wasn't
working during the Christmas holidays
and Yasmeen had been able to plan a few
days of winter fun. But she was worried
that this week would be a bit of a let-
down after their action-packed days at
camp. And what would the girls think of
Yasmeen's little flat?

The intercom buzzed and Yasmeen
nearly toppled off her bar stool. She slid
along the wooden floor to answer it.

"Hi!" she shouted in excitement, before
holding the receiver away from her ear
because of the shrieking at the other end.
It was Oralie, Amber and Rose. Amber's
mum had given them all a lift. Yasmeen
buzzed them in and raced to meet them
at the door. "It's so good to see you!"

she cried, squeezing them all tightly in a group hug.

"I'M GETTING A PUPPY!" cried Oralie. "Sorry, I mean, hello and how are you and stuff like that, but I'm SO EXCITED about the puppy and it's all thanks to Rose letting us have Wriggly to stay in the summer—"

"This is all Oralie has talked about for the *entire* journey," said Amber with a smile.

"We put the radio on in the end but she talked over it," said Rose.

Yasmeen laughed. "I can't wait to hear all about it!" A big Old English Sheepdog padded over to greet the girls. She had a shaggy white and grey coat that covered her eyes.

"This is Mabel," said Yasmeen.

"Aww, hello," said Rose, putting out her hand for Mabel to sniff, which Mabel did before happily sitting down at Rose's feet.

"I think she likes you!" said Yasmeen.

Yasmeen led the girls through to a room with a wooden floor, which was lounge, dining room and kitchen all in one.

"You can put your stuff in my room but there isn't enough space to sleep in there, so we'll be sleeping in here. In fact, we'll be doing everything in here."

"Wow! Your flat is so cool! I've never been in a flat before. I want a place *exactly* like this when I grow up," said Oralie. The room was decorated in black and white, with a fluffy grey rug in the middle. A breakfast bar separated the kitchen from the living space.

Amber looked around, open-mouthed. "You've got a huge TV! And bar stools!" The mums were sitting and chatting on them at that very moment.

"But where are all your things?" asked

Rose. "It's so *tidy*!"

"Well, it's just me and Mum, so we don't need a lot of stuff. And Mabel, of course. But she doesn't run around like she used to. And luckily our flat's downstairs, so she can go out in the garden whenever she wants to."

The girls peeped outside and saw a square of neatly trimmed grass, dotted with winter flowers in pots.

"I love your garden!" said Oralie.

"I was worried that it might all seem a bit ... you know ... small."

Amber laughed. "You live in London, Yasmeen! It's so exciting. We saw red buses and Tube stations on the way here."

Yasmeen's mum brought out a tall jug of blackcurrant squash and Yasmeen poured a glass for each of the girls.

"I guess there *is* a lot to do around here, even if we haven't got a lot of room. The best news is, Mum says we can go to the Winter Warmer festival tomorrow!"

"What's the Winter Warmer festival?" asked Rose. She'd never heard of it, but it sounded like something magical and fun.

Yasmeen took a flier from the noticeboard on her kitchen wall and passed it to Rose. "It's like a Christmas fair but mega big and with rides and stalls and music and stuff."

"NO WAY, that sounds ace!" said Oralie, looking at the flier.

"Before we catch up on all the latest news, did you all remember your bracelets?" asked Yasmeen, pushing up her sleeve to reveal hers, which was silver, after her surname, Silver. All the girls happened to have names that were related to a precious metal: Rose Gold, Yasmeen Silver, Amber Beau and Oralie Sands.

"Yes!" chorused the others, who were all wearing their bracelets especially. The girls put down their glasses of blackcurrant, crossed their arms and held hands in a circle, the metal clinking together.

"Make new friends but keep the old, Amber, Silver, Rose and Gold," chanted Yasmeen, and the others joined in.

Rose smiled. "I don't think we're new friends any more, are we?"

"Definitely not. We're old friends now," agreed Oralie.

It was their special rhyme for special friends. Now that they were here with her, Yasmeen no longer felt nervous.

Nothing would go wrong. They were going to have the *best* time.

Chapter 2

Winter Wildlife

Amber's mum left after finishing her cup of tea and checking that the girls were OK. Soon after, Yasmeen's mum brought their coats through. "Right, we've still got time to go to Rose's exhibition. Don't forget your gloves and hats — it's cold out there!"

Rose was a talented artist — she'd

even won an art competition a few weeks before. As well as winning some professional art materials, part of Rose's prize was to have her drawing displayed in a London gallery and made into a Christmas card. The gallery was only a short bus ride away from Yasmeen's flat, so they had decided to all go and see her drawing together before Rose went with her family.

They sat upstairs at the front of the bus, taking up the two front double seats, with Yasmeen's mum behind them staring out of the window. Yasmeen turned to try and catch Mum's eye but she didn't notice. She seemed quieter than usual. The girls chatted all the way, catching up on some of the news they'd missed.

"We said over email that we all had news to share. Let's go round and everyone can share one thing each. Rose, do you want to start?" suggested Yasmeen.

Rose smiled. "You all know my news – I won this art competition! That's it! I'm so glad you can all come with me to see it – before my parents even."

"I bet you're going to be a famous artist when you are older and have your work exhibited all around the world.

Will you take us on holiday in your private jet?" Oralie wiggled her glasses up and down.

Rose laughed. "Yes, OK!"

Amber looked thoughtful. "I do have something to share. It's good news, but I might save it until the end of the week, if that's OK."

"Of course," said Yasmeen.

Oralie buried her face in her hands. "NO WAY! I don't like waiting for secrets!"

The girls all burst out laughing again, so loudly that Yasmeen's mum looked up. "Who wants to press the button? This is our stop coming up."

"Ooh, me, me, me!" said Oralie, pressing the red button on the pole. The sign changed to *BUS STOPPING* and she giggled. "I never get to travel on

buses at home."

The girls piled off the bus and on to
the pavement. The gallery was right near
the bus stop – just a few metres along
the street. It was a big, impressive place
with cream-coloured stone pillars outside
and a large poster introducing the Winter
Wildlife exhibition. Yasmeen's mum took
photos of them all leaning against the

columns, and then a special one of Rose by herself next to the exhibition poster. Then they went up the steps, inside, and up to the front desk. The woman behind the desk smiled as they approached.

"We are here to see our friend's drawing. She is a *prize-winner*," announced Oralie, and the girls laughed while Rose went a little bit pink with embarrassment.

The woman behind the desk was really kind. She leaned over and shook Rose's hand and said, "I'm honoured to meet you!" Then she passed them all a leaflet with a map on the back and pointed to it with a shiny blue fingernail. "The children's Christmas card competition display is in the north gallery, just here. I'm afraid you will need to walk past some of the adults' work on the way, but some of it is quite good."

The theme of the exhibition was Winter Wildlife, and there were lots of penguins and polar bears, and even some more interesting takes on the theme.

"Which one's your favourite?" asked Yasmeen.

Amber stopped by a giant snow leopard made of recycled materials. "I like this one. The longer you look at it, the more you see. Look, there are bottle tops, plastic bags, even some old toy cars!"

"This is my favourite," said Yasmeen's mum, stopping in front of a ladder in the middle of the room. It was painted white, and a large paper lantern hung from the ceiling above. It was covered in tiny white birds, made from polystyrene balls and feathers.

"I love all the feathers," said Amber. "It looks as if it's going to fly away."

Yasmeen's mum nodded. "Yes, and all the white together is really effective. White's my favourite colour."

They all discussed whether white was actually a real colour or not as they were on their way to the north gallery, where the winners from the children's art competition were all displayed on one big wall. Each age category had one winner and two runners-up, and everything was framed and labelled. The pictures looked like real works of art.

"They are all really good," said Yasmeen.

"Here's yours, Rose!" said Amber.

Rose's entry was a pastel picture of a robin. She had used coloured pencils to

show the details of all the feathers, and
to draw its shiny black eyes. In places,
the lines were careful and fine, and in
other areas the colours were blended. It

was clear that she had spent hours on it.

"They are all really good, but I can see why yours won," whispered Oralie.

"It's amazing," said Yasmeen, with tears in her eyes. She felt really proud of her friend.

Yasmeen's mum took more photos, including a couple of Rose next to her framed picture and a couple of the four of them together.

"I think we'll be coming to plenty more of your exhibitions," said Amber, and they all agreed. Rose would definitely be a famous artist one day.

Chapter 3

Noodles and twinkly lights

After the gallery, Yasmeen's mum took
them to a noodle bar. It was packed with
people and they squeezed on to wooden
benches around a little table in the
basement. They ate big bowls of delicious
steaming noodles, filled dumplings
and spring rolls. By the time they had
finished and made their way outside, it

was dark and starting to get really cold. They walked down Regent Street to look at the Christmas lights with full, warm tummies.

Way above their heads, lights stretched across the street and as far as they could see behind them. The window displays glowed with bright colours and more twinkly lights.

Rose wrapped her scarf over her nose and mouth to try and keep warm. Above the green wool, her eyes were wide, and when she spoke, her voice was muffled. "I'm starting to feel Christmassy now I've seen the lights. My dad puts loads of lights outside the front of our house every year – we even have a reindeer with his sleigh … but I've never seen Christmas lights as big as this!"

Yasmeen, who was also hiding behind

her scarf, nodded. "I love the lights too, even though we don't celebrate Christmas. We do a bit of shopping but it's nothing major. Chinese New Year is our big celebration."

"We've just celebrated Diwali," said Amber, "which is a whole festival of lights. We sometimes have fireworks

in the garden. I
like the Christmas
holidays too, but more because we're all
on holiday together rather than the fact
that it's Christmas. We buy all the ready-
made food from the supermarket and
have a film-fest."

Oralie didn't seem to be feeling the
cold like the others, and she skipped

along with her hood down and her gloves swinging from her sleeves from their elastic. "My family LOVES Christmas. It's all about the food. If I see my family in France, then we eat all day — we have about ten million courses."

They reached their bus stop and Amber sat down on the little sloped bench. Rose and Yasmeen just about managed to squeeze on but there was no room for Oralie. "That's OK," she said, "I'm too excited to sit down, anyway. Oh — look at that poster!"

The girls turned to their right and examined the enormous poster. It was a magical snowy scene with an ice-skating rink surrounded by little wooden huts and fairground rides. In blue lettering at the top of the poster was written,

WINTER WARMER FESTIVAL.

Yasmeen traced a gloved finger over one of the little ice skaters. "Wow. I can't believe we're going there tomorrow! I'm looking forward to the ice-skating the most. I can already roller skate but I've never been on the ice before. Do you think it will be any different?"

Amber giggled. "I've done it a few times and I fell over loads but it was fun! We can pick each other up! And we could all go on the big wheel! I bet we'll have a great view..."

"What are the little fairy tale cottages for?" asked Rose.

"Those are market stalls," said Yasmeen. "They all sell stuff like crafts and candy canes and doughnuts."

Oralie sniffed the air. "Mmmm, doughnuts! I can almost smell them now. I'm going to buy about ten. I think doughnuts might be my favourite Christmas smell."

"Doughnuts aren't Christmassy," said Amber.

"They are if you sprinkle cinnamon on them," said Oralie wisely. "Cinnamon makes *everything* Christmassy. So, actually, maybe cinnamon is my favourite Christmas smell."

"I like pine needles," said Rose.

"Gingerbread," said Amber. "What about you, Yasmeen?"

Yasmeen thought for a second. "You might think it's odd, but ... apples."

"Apples! OK, you're going to have to explain that one," said Oralie

"It's a Chinese thing. We sometimes wrap them up and give them to people at this time of year, and they look really pretty. They sometimes even have Christmas messages printed on them. So now just the smell of apples makes me think of Christmas."

Oralie jumped up from the bench and pulled her mittens on. Even she was getting cold now. She looked at the display. "Three minutes until the bus comes. Let's do more winter favourites, where we give a category and then say our favourite thing. I'll start. Favourite ... winter food?"

"Soup!" said Rose.

"Those noodles we just ate," said Oralie.

"Mithai! They're Indian sweets. I especially like the almond ones," said Amber.

"Apples again!" said Yasmeen.

"I would love to see one of these Christmas apples," said Rose.

"I'll make sure I give you one each before you go," said Yasmeen. "Will you help me remember, Mum?"

Yasmeen's mum was standing next to them but didn't seem to be listening. She sneezed all of a sudden. Her face was pale and her eyes looked a bit pink.

"Are you OK, Mum?" asked Yasmeen. Now that she was looking closely, she could see that her mum didn't look well at all.

"I'm not feeling *quite* right," admitted her mum. "I've got a sore throat and a bit of a temperature, but I should be fine. I just need a good night's sleep."

But Yasmeen was worried. Her mum was *never* ill. It was only the two of them at home and Mum was the one who looked after Yasmeen, not the other way around!

Finally the bus arrived and the girls got on, still chattering about winter food. Yasmeen watched her mum. She hoped that she was right and would feel better in the morning. What would they do if she didn't?

Chapter 4

Best Laid Plans

In the morning, the girls woke up early, bubbling with excitement. They stayed in their beds, watching the TV on low and talking over it about their Winter Warmer plans.

But Yasmeen didn't join in. She watched her mum's bedroom door, and she watched the clock. Was Mum going to wake up feeling better? It was eight o'clock, and Mum was *always* up by now. She said she was an early riser – programmed to get up for work even in the holidays – so why hadn't she even opened her door?

Yasmeen got out of bed and poured a glass of orange juice, then carried it carefully to her mum's bedroom

and pushed open the door. Mum was snuggled under the covers but she poked her head out.

"Morning, love," she croaked.

Yasmeen sat down next to her. Mum didn't look better. In fact, she looked *very* poorly. Yasmeen laid her hand against her mum's forehead, like Mum did for her when she was ill. Mum felt hot, but she was shivering under the blanket.

"Can I get you anything?" asked Yasmeen.

"Can you pass me the tablets from my dressing table?" replied her mum.

Yasmeen got up and passed her the foil packet of tablets, and she swallowed two with a sip of orange juice before looking at Yasmeen sadly. "Yasmeen, love, I'm so sorry but I feel terrible. I'm not going to be able to take you to the Winter Warmer festival."

Yasmeen burst into tears. How could this happen? She grabbed a tissue from Mum's bedside cabinet and wiped her eyes. It wasn't Mum's fault but it was just so unfair. "But what are we going to do?" she asked.

Mum patted Yasmeen's arm. "I think it would be best for everyone if we call Amber's mum and ask her to collect everyone."

"No!" wailed Yasmeen. "I can't send them home. We've all been looking forward to today so much."

"Well, if you stayed here, you'd have to entertain yourselves. And you wouldn't be able to go anywhere, because I just need to sleep. I'm so sorry. Why don't you ask them and see what they say?" she added after a pause.

★

The girls knew straight away from Yasmeen's tear-stained face that something wasn't right. She explained the whole situation and told them all about not being able to go to the Winter Warmer festival.

And, actually, they took it better than she had thought.

Oralie didn't need any time to think about it. "We stay. Obviously."

Amber agreed. "Did we give up when we had to hide Wriggly at camp? No, and we won't give up now!"

Yasmeen shook her head and Rose put her arm around her. "We're good at making the best of things. And having fun together. We can still enjoy the rest of the weekend, even without the Winter Warmer festival."

Amber got out of bed and rolled up her sleeping bag. "This *isn't* a disaster. Actually, it doesn't matter at all. The festival would have been fun, but we can have just as much fun here."

"And we can look after your mum," added Rose.

So it was decided: they would all stay. And their first task was to make sure that Yasmeen's mum was comfortable.

"Has she got enough pillows?" said Rose.

"She has to drink lots of fluids," said Oralie. "That what my mum always tells me."

"My mum gives me a syrup made from lemon juice, cinnamon and honey. Shall I make some?" suggested Amber.

Yasmeen got an extra pillow from her bedroom, and heated up Mum's wheat bag in the microwave. She wetted a clean flannel under the hot tap and wrung it out, then put it all on a tray with Amber's special cure and some eucalyptus oil and took it all through to Mum's bedroom.

Yasmeen wiped the flannel across Mum's forehead and sprinkled a few drops of essential oil on her duvet. "This should help, Mum. Here, have some of Amber's special syrup."

Mum swallowed a spoonful of the lemon mixture. "That tastes delicious but I'm worried about you all playing nursemaid to me. Are you going to be OK staying inside?"

"We'll be fine. The girls don't mind about missing the festival. You get some sleep and get well soon."

Yasmeen kissed her mum and closed the door gently behind her.

"I think she's going to be OK," she said to the girls. She tried to smile but was finding it difficult today. Why did the best plans always seem to go wrong?

Oralie clapped her hands together and jumped up. Yasmeen knew that look – it meant that she had a idea. "Remember Camp BigToes and how we decorated our boring old room?" said Oralie excitedly.

The girls all nodded. They had made it into a pirate paradise and even won a prize. That was how they came to have their special bracelets – they'd bought them with their prize money.

Oralie sprang into action, rolling up the sleeping mats and pushing back the sofas. "Well, let's do the same thing now. While your mum gets some rest, Yasmeen, let's turn your flat into our very own Winter Warmer festival!"

Chapter 5

A Stepladder and Some Fairy Lights

Oralie waved the Winter Warmer flier from the noticeboard under their noses. "We need to recreate all this ... in here." She swept her arms around to indicate the flat.

"We're going to struggle with the big wheel, to be fair," said Amber.

"I know, but there's loads of other stuff we can do. We should start by making the flat *look* right. Have you got any decorations, Yasmeen?"

"There might be something in the cleaning cupboard out in the hall."

Amber took out a bundled up string of fairy lights. There were also some red and gold wall hangings and some Chinese New Year lanterns. "It's a bit early to put those up," said Yasmeen, doubtfully. Apart from a spider guarding her web in the top corner of the cupboard, there was nothing else. Oralie stroked her chin and pointed to an old wooden stepladder behind the ironing board. "I've got an idea. That looks perfect. Can you help me get it out, Amber?" The girls struggled to lift the ladder between them.

"I don't know if Mum would want us climbing up ladders while she's in bed," said Yasmeen.

"Don't worry; we're not going to climb it. Remember the ladder with the birds in the gallery? This is going to be our Winter Warmer artwork!"

They managed to carry the ladder through to the living room and Oralie unfolded it near the window. They wrapped the fairy lights around like they had seen in the gallery and it did look quite pretty.

"Now we can tie on more decorations and even balance stuff on the rungs of the ladder," said Amber.

Yasmeen looked thoughtful. "That does sound nice but Mum's not into colourful decorations. She likes things to match!"

Rose thought for a moment and looked

around the tidy, polished flat. "Your Mum did say at the exhibition that her favourite colour was white. So that could be our colour scheme. White, with maybe a hint of silver."

"But where are we going to get the decorations from?" said Yasmeen. "The shops are miles away. And we can't go out on our own."

"We'll make them," said Amber. "You've got plain white paper, haven't you? Scissors? Glue? And foil?"

Yasmeen nodded.

"And I bet if we raid the recycling bin there will be other stuff we can use. Remember the snow leopard made from recycled stuff?"

Yasmeen nodded and had a rummage. "There is some newspaper here and a couple of old packets and jars."

"Perfect!" said Rose. "Let's start with paper chains. We can make those from newspaper and they'll look really good."

Oralie followed instructions and began cutting a sheet of newspaper into equal size strips.

Amber picked up a strip and curled it into a ring. She fixed it with sticky tape and began threading a new strip through. "I love making these. I could sit here for hours doing this."

"I do too. Let's each make a short chain and join them together. Race you!"

Amber and Oralie giggled and paper-chained furiously. Rose assessed the rest of the recycling materials.

Yasmeen watched her. "I bet you're going to make something really impressive, aren't you? I wish I knew how to make something crafty. Oooh, actually I do!" A thought occurred to Yasmeen and she crossed the room and opened a drawer full of wrapping paper and birthday cards. She pulled out a packet of white tissue paper with silver flecks. She squealed. "This is perfect! I do know how to make something crafty – Mum and I used to make loads of these when I was little."

Yasmeen sat at the breakfast bar folding the tissue paper forwards and backwards like a fan.

"What are you making?" called

Oralie, without looking up from her paper chain.

"You'll see," said Yasmeen, cutting the

end into a rounded shape.

Oralie laughed. "Mysterious! What about you, Rose?"

Rose had also embarked on a craft activity, curling strips of white paper with scissors. "I'm not sure yet. I'm making it up as I go along."

With everyone concentrating, the room went quiet.

"We need some music!" said Amber. "I know – favourite ... winter song?"

Yasmeen answered straight away. "'In the Bleak Midwinter'. We sing it at school. It makes me think of cold snowy days. I cry every time I hear it."

"Yasmeen! Everything makes you cry!" said Rose.

"They are happy tears."

"Well all this decorating makes me think of 'Deck the Halls'," said Oralie, coughing to warm up her singing voice. *"Deck the Halls with boughs of holly—"*

Yasmeen flapped her hands. "No, Oralie, whatever you do, don't sing!"

Oralie looked offended. "What? My singing voice isn't that bad! *Fa-la-la-la-la, la-la-la-la—"*

Suddenly, Mabel raised her doggy nose into the air and joined in. "It sounded something like, "Woo awoo awoo," and it was loud, although sort of in time to the song.

The girls all clamped their hands over their ears.

"That is why I said not to sing. Mabel likes to join in," said Yasmeen. The girls

all laughed and sang the "fa-la-la-la-la's" and Mabel howled noisily along.

"Shhh, Mabel – you'll wake Mum! We'd better stick with the radio. Yasmeen switched on the radio at low volume and went to check on Mum, but it was OK – she was still sleeping.

The radio played lots of songs they knew and Mabel only sang along if they did. She plodded between them and occasionally got tangled in the paper chain. After twenty minutes of intense craft activity, the girls put down their scissors and glue. They stretched their fingers.

"Phew! This crafting business is hard work." Oralie stood up and unfurled the paper chain. It was long enough to drape around the room and there would be enough left over for the ladder-tree.

Rose had made a little white bird like the ones in the gallery. Its body was a ball of polystyrene packaging and it had curled paper strips for a tail. The others loved it so much that she had to show them how to make them. Soon ten little birds perched on the ladder.

Yasmeen fluffed out her tissue paper folds into a giant white pompom flower.

"Wow, it's beautiful!" said Rose.

"It should go right at the top of the ladder," said Amber. As the tallest, she only had to climb up three steps before she could hang it from the ceiling.

Rose stopped and gazed around the room. Such simple decorations, but all together they were striking. "Wow. This all looks amazing."

"Yes, thank you. We do have our very own Winter Warmer festival. I'm feeling better already," said Yasmeen.

Oralie shook her head vigorously. "But it isn't finished yet. No, no no! We're only just getting started..."

Chapter 6

Snowmen, Aliens and a Squid

"Decorations are just one part of it. What about all the other things?" Oralie ran her finger along the colourful writing on the flier.

FOOD! MUSIC! GIFTS! ICE SKATING FUN!

"Well," said Yasmeen, "food is easy. We have lots of that. We just need to Winter Warmify it. Why don't we decorate some cupcakes?"

Yasmeen took a packet of cakes from the cupboard and opened a drawer full of boxes and tubes. "All our baking stuff is in here. We have icing sugar and icing pens..."

Rose joined her. "Ooh, look. You even have marshmallows and silver balls.

I know what we can make: snowman cupcakes!"

"There are twelve cakes — that's three each," said Oralie.

Amber mixed up some white icing in a bowl, and they spooned it over all the cakes.

Rose showed them how to ice noses, eyes, scarves and buttons. "How did you get so good at that?" said Yasmeen as she squeezed icing out of the pen. "It's really hard!"

"Practice makes perfect, I guess," said Rose.

"As usual, yours looks like it belongs in a gallery," said Oralie.

"And they are white, so Yasmeen's mum will approve!" said Amber.

After they had each made a snowman cake, they began to get *really* creative.

Oralie added brown floppy ears and a pink tongue to her next cupcake. "It's a snow puppy. Did I mention I'M GETTING A PUPPY?"

"Once or twice!" said Amber. "Mine's a snow woman. This is her hair." She carefully piped orange curly locks down the side of the cake.

Rose gave her cake dark patches like a snow leopard. Yasmeen added loads of eyes and tentacles to hers.

"Erm, what is that, Yasmeen? A squid?" asked Oralie.

The girls all giggled. "No! It's the cute alien from that film – *Planet Freezy*," said Yasmeen, giving the alien some blue mittens.

"*Planet Freezy*? I thought I had watched *every* film that was ever made, but I've never heard of *Planet Freezy*," said Amber.

"Then you're missing out. It's about this alien who comes down to earth in December and sees it all snowy. He spends the day sledging and throwing snowballs with a little boy and his family and then he tries to make it snow on his own planet..." Yasmeen's eyes began to fill with tears. "I can't explain how good it is — we have to watch it."

"OK, so everyone else's favourite ... cosy winter film?" said Oralie.

By the time they had all shared their favourite films, they had decorated all of the cakes. As well as snowmen, aliens and puppies they had elves, frogs and even an actual squid.

While the icing was drying, the girls took Mabel for a walk around the communal gardens, peeking at people's decorations as they went. There were

wreaths on some doors, sparkly Christmas trees and cut-out paper snowflakes on the windows.

"I think our decorations are the best though," said Amber.

When they got back, Yasmeen checked on her mum, who was still fast asleep. Then they each tucked into a snowman cake and a hot chocolate, which Yasmeen made in the microwave.

The cakes, especially the snowman bit, were delicious. They blew on the hot chocolate to cool it and then took little sips. "Mmm, lovely. I can't imagine anything at the Winter Warmer festival tasting this good, can you?" said Oralie.

Yasmeen sighed. "It *is* delicious, but I still can't help thinking about how much fun it would have been. I was really looking forward to the ice skating."

The girls picked at the crumbs of their cakes until Amber stood up with a grin on her face. "I have the *best* idea. Do you have any paper plates?"

"I . . . think so," said Yasmeen, getting up to search in the kitchen cupboard. "Why?"

"We're going to go ice skating after all," said Oralie.

Chapter 7

Ice Skating

Oralie flapped her hands excitedly. "When I was in nursery, we used to skate on paper plates. Yasmeen's got such a shiny floor, that I thought it might work. Shall we try it?"

Yasmeen rolled up the fluffy rug and they pushed the sofa back against the wall. "We have loads of room now. Who's going to go first? Oralie?"

Oralie shook her head. "Go on, Amber, you like extreme sports!"

Amber laughed and stood on the paper plates. By sliding her feet one at a time she travelled from one end of the room to the other. "It works! It's just like ice skating!"

Now the others wanted a go too – they tried paper plates first, and then had a go with cushions, dusters and even old tissue boxes. Dusters were the fastest. "We're even polishing the floor as we do it – your mum will be pleased," said Rose.

Amber stood with one foot stretched out behind her and her arms to the side. "Let's try figure skating next!"

"Don't all the ice skating poses have

names?" said Yasmeen. "I think the one you're doing now is called the spread eagle."

Rose stuck out her elbows like chicken wings. "This one's the chicken!" she laughed.

Oralie kneeled on all fours. "This is the new puppy pose!" Mabel padded over and stood next to Oralie in an identical pose, which made everyone laugh even more.

"Mabel wants to join in!" said Amber, collapsing in a happy heap on the floor, pulling a throw from the sofa as she went.

For a minute Amber lay on the cosy throw, feeling snug. Then she sat on one corner of the blanket and adjusted it so it pooled around her. "Someone give me a pull!" Oralie took the free corner and dragged her round the shiny floor in circles until she was red and breathless.

When they had all had a go at blanket sledging and their cheeks were pink, they piled on to the sofa.

"I actually think that was way more fun than proper ice skating would have been," said Rose.

Amber nodded. "You're right – it wasn't cold or wet, and there was no one else in the way. Have you seen how busy those ice rinks get at this time of year?"

Yasmeen smiled. "Who needs ice skating when you have best friends? And Mabel got to join in the fun, too. Did you like the ice skating, Oralie? Oralie. . .?"

Oralie had stopped listening to the conversation and was staring out of the window with a surprised look on her face. "Is that what I think it is?"

The others turned to look. The sky was darkening outside but some large, white flakes were floating down and settling on the grass. "SNOW!" they shrieked together, rushing to the window.

"Maybe it's going to snow so much that we'll be snowed in for days and can do indoor ice skating for a whole week," said Amber.

"Maybe it will snow for so long that we'll miss school in January," said Rose.

"*In the bleak midwinter—*" Oralie started singing.

"No, stop!" cried Yasmeen, but it was too late – Mabel had already started howling along. "OWOO, WOW WOW."

"Shhh, Mabel!" they all said, giggling and stroking to soothe her.

At that moment, Yasmeen's mum finally emerged from her bedroom, rubbing her eyes.

Yasmeen ran to give her a hug. "Wow, Mum, you've slept for six whole hours!"

"I'm feeling a bit better now. Maybe we can—"

Yasmeen's mum gasped when she saw what the girls had done. She stood there for a moment with her hands at her cheeks, taking in the paper chains, the decorated stepladder and the pile of cupcakes.

Yasmeen chewed her lip. Mum didn't really like a lot of clutter in the flat. "Do you mind?" said Yasmeen. "We didn't stick anything on the walls."

"It's magical!" said her mum. "Aren't you all clever?" She took a tissue and wiped the tears from her eyes.

"Now we know where Yasmeen gets her crying from!" said Oralie.

Yasmeen's mum laughed. "You girls must be getting hungry. I'm not sure I'm well enough to cook tonight, so why don't we order a pizza?"

Chapter 8

Planet Freezy

The girls got together the plates, napkins and drinks so that they could eat the pizza in front of a film.

"Great! We have everything we could ever want. And now for the best bit!" Yasmeen reached for the remote control and flicked through some films on the TV. "Found it!"

"What's that?"

"*Planet Freezy*, of course!"

Planet Freezy was as good as Yasmeen had told them. The girls and Mabel sat squeezed together on one sofa with sleeping bags and blankets tucked around them. Yasmeen's mum lay on the other sofa, looking a lot better. They had three slices of pizza each as well as garlic bread and potato wedges, and cried their way through a whole box of tissues.

Afterwards, Oralie shook her head slowly. "That bit when he saves the mouse in the snow was too much for me."

"I know," said Yasmeen. "Now do you see why it's my favourite?"

The girls all nodded.

"Thank you for being my pillow, Mabel," said Amber. She had been resting her head on the big dog for most of the film.

Rose cuddled Mabel. "Mabel gives the most cuddly cuddles. Wriggly's cuddles are lovely, of course," she added loyally, "but he *is* very . . . wriggly. Mabel is the most cuddly."

"I wonder what *my* puppy will be like," said Oralie. "I think we're getting a pug. Are they cuddly?"

Amber gave Oralie a cuddle. "I'm sure your puppy will be cuddly and always up to mischief, just like you!"

Yasmeen's mum went for another little lie down, and the girls put the lights on inside but kept the curtains open so that they could watch the snow falling while they chatted all evening about pets, crafts and favourite winter things. It really did feel like a Warm Winter.

Chapter 9

Au Revoir

The next morning, the girls slumped on the sofa waiting for Rose's mum to arrive. Their packed bags were in a heap on the floor next to them.

"I can't believe it's Sunday already and we have to go home," said Rose.

Yasmeen's mum, who was feeling

much better now, laughed. "And I can't believe that you had such a good time when you didn't go anywhere or do anything!"

"But we did!" said Oralie. "We spent the day at our very own Winter Warmer festival and even went ice skating."

"And we went to Planet Freezy," said Amber.

"And we discovered that it doesn't matter *where* we are as long as we're together," said Rose.

Yasmeen's mum laughed. "You've forgotten one important thing before you go. Yasmeen, you asked me to remind you about the gifts."

"Oh yes!" cried Yasmeen. She ran out of the room and the other girls began unzipping their bags to find the presents that they'd brought along.

Yasmeen reappeared with three beautifully-wrapped spheres. One was yellow gold, one was rose gold and one was orange. The girls didn't need name labels to know whose was whose.

Yasmeen watched the girls pick them up and ooh and ah over the shiny wrapping paper. "Can you guess what they are?"

"Are we allowed to shake them?" asked Oralie, raising her present in the air.

Yasmeen stopped her. "No, don't shake them! Smell them!"

Amber pressed the orange sphere up to her nose and inhaled. "Apples!"

Rose did the same. "You're right — they *do* smell of Christmas!"

"Are they special Chinese apples?" asked Oralie.

Yasmeen's mum laughed again. "No, just regular apples!"

The intercom buzzed and she stood up. "That will be your mum, Rose. I'll go and let her in while you open the rest of your presents."

"Mine's not really a present. It's just a card," said Rose, handing them each an envelope.

Oralie ripped hers open straight away. It was one of the special Christmas cards printed with Rose's artwork. "This isn't *just* a card! This is an amazing work of art! I'm going to put mine on the wall at home."

"I might keep mine in the envelope. I'll sell it for millions of pounds when you're rich and famous," said Amber, but she was opening the envelope as she said it.

"But, Rose, you only had four of these cards. Are you sure you want to give them away?" asked Yasmeen.

"Yes! There was one for me and one for each of my best friends. Four was the perfect amount!"

Oralie gave everyone a framed copy of a photo of the four of them from camp. They were arm-in-arm, grinning at the camera.

"Oh, look at the frames – they are our colours!" said Rose.

Oralie had even written their special rhyme on the back.

Make new friends but keep the old;
Amber, Silver, Rose and Gold.

"Mine's a late Diwali gift!" said Amber, thrusting long, flat rectangular packages into all their hands.

Rose opened hers first. "A calendar! With a different puppy for each month! Thanks, Amber."

The others all had the same gift. Amber interrupted their thank yous by saying, "Turn to February!"

The girls all flipped the pages over to February, where Amber had marked the third Monday with a big red circle.

They all looked at her quizzically and Amber clapped her hands together. "The secret I was going to tell you on the bus is that... Mum says you can stay at ours in February half term!

"Yay!" they cried. This was the best news. Every time they got together, it became even more difficult to imagine a holiday spent apart.

The girls hugged one another in a tight circle. It had been such a special reunion, and now they had a visit to Amber's house to look forward to, which was only a couple of months away. They would all be marking off the days on their new calendars!

Turn over for a sneak peak at another
Rose Gold adventure:

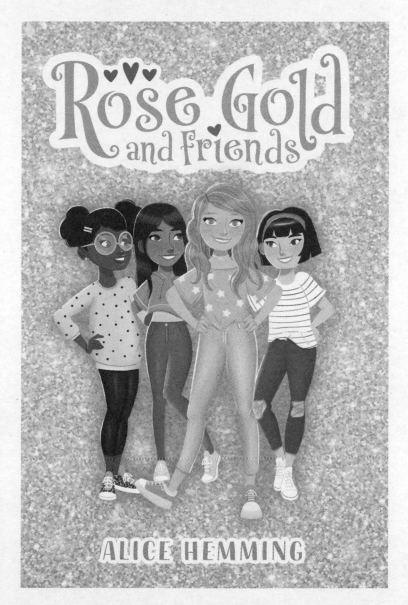

ROSE GOLD
and Friends

ALICE HEMMING

Chapter 1

Camp BigToes

Rose's Mum gave her a goodbye hug. "Have an *amazing* time at summer camp. I'm sure you will!"

Rose wished that *she* could be as confident. She had been on a school trip before, but just for one night. Camp would be *three whole nights* without anyone she knew. Questions whirled around her brain. *What would the food be like? Would she make any friends?* And the biggest question of all, *Would Wriggly be OK?* She gave her fluffy cockapoo one last cuddle, then waved goodbye as he trotted off on the lead with Mum and Dad. Tears pricked at Rose's eyes. Saying goodbye to Wriggly was hard. He probably thought he was going on a nice walk through the woods, but her parents were actually taking him to the kennels around the corner. They were going to a wedding and couldn't take him with them. Mum and Dad said that the kennels were like summer camp for dogs but Rose didn't like the thought of being away from him.

Rose shook the thought from her mind. It was a sunny day, she was here at summer camp and she was going to try to have fun. A person with a blue Camp Bickrose T-Shirt and a swingy high ponytail bounded over. "Hi, Rose, my name is Jess and I'm going to be your Group Leader here at Bickrose Hall. I'll show you the ropes and make sure you're in the right place at the right time."

Jess beckoned another girl over. "This is Oralie, she's one of your cabin mates. She got here early, so already knows where everything is. She'll show you to your room."

As soon as Rose saw Oralie she felt better. Oralie had red-and-blue striped round glasses and a big smile. Her black hair stuck out around her head in a beautiful frizz. She looked like a lot of fun.

"Hi," said Rose, smiling back shyly. As she followed Oralie to their cabin, Oralie talked all the way. "I got here early because my dad is working at the camp. He's only here until Wednesday, though, so at least I get one day all by myself. He has promised that I can pretend I don't know him the rest of the time!"

As Oralie talked, Rose looked around her, taking it all in. Bickrose Hall was a big mansion house set out in the countryside, surrounded by woodland.

"This is the girls' accommodation," said Oralie, pointing to the three log cabins to the right of the main building. "Each cabin has two rooms."

Oralie led them to the first cabin, through the main door and then into the left-hand room. It was small and comfortable-looking with yellow walls and bright bedspreads. Sun streamed through the window, shining light on to the two bunk beds on each side of the room. There was a chest of drawers at the foot of each bed, and a storage box and metal locker on the wall for each girl.

Oralie spread out her arms in an excited welcome. "This is going to be our home for the next three nights! I haven't put my stuff on any of the beds yet," she continued, looking at the bunk beds. "I didn't know where people would want to sleep. Do you snore?"

"I don't think so," said Rose. Even if she did, how would she ever know?

"Great! Would you like to be my

bunkmate, then?"

"I'd love to," Rose said, pleased that she'd made such a fun friend already.

"Top or bottom?" asked Oralie

"I don't mind," said Rose.

Oralie put her hands on her hips. "I really, *really* don't mind. You decide!"

"Then, I guess ... bottom?"

Rose unzipped her holdall and began putting her leggings and T-shirts into the drawers. Then the door opened and two more faces peeped in.

"Is this 1A?" asked the first girl, who had black shiny hair in a bob and a serious face. "I'm Yasmeen, by the way."

"... and I'm Amber," said the other girl, wearing a baseball cap with long black hair tucked underneath.

"Yes, this is 1A – are you our roommates?" asked Oralie.

They nodded. "Jess sent us here. She
said we have five minutes to unpack
before the camp tour begins."

While Amber and Yasmeen put their
things on the other bunk beds, they all
talked non-stop, trying to find out as
much as they could about each other
before the tour began. Rose knew she
was being quieter than usual, but she was
still feeling a little overwhelmed by it all.

They heard Jess bang on the door of the room opposite before banging on their door too. "Time for the tour, everybody! This is your chance to find out where everything is. Ask me anything!"

Jess led their cabin around the grounds, telling them anything and everything they needed to know. The girls in 1B seemed nice enough, but were a couple of years older than everyone in Rose's cabin and stuck together in a giggling group.

There was so much to see at Camp Bickrose: art and music studios, a high ropes course, an archery centre, tennis courts, even an outdoor swimming pool. Amber's eyes lit up when she saw the pool. "Will we be going in there?"

"If it's hot enough," said Jess. Then, pointing to a dirt track outside the

grounds, she said, "There's a farm over
there. They have all sorts of animals,
even llamas. Hence the llama trekking
option on Sunday."

A murmur of excitement spread across
the group. *Everyone* wanted to do the
llama trekking!

Rose was starting to feel hot with her
hoody on and unzipped it. There was
something bulky in the pocket – what
was it? Pulling it out, she saw: it was
one of Wriggly's favourite dog chews,
left over from her last walk with him
at home. That was only this morning,
but somehow it felt like for ever ago. As
she tied her hoody around her waist she
wondered if she was going to be OK
here at Camp Bickrose, however lovely
people seemed to be.

After they had toured the grounds,

they got to go inside Bickrose Hall itself. There was a big dining hall where they would eat all their meals, a TV room with big comfy chairs and sofas, and a games room with table tennis and pool tables. "And that's the camp shop," said Jess, waving in the direction of a small shop stocked with sweets, chocolates, souvenirs and gifts.

"Your parents have given me your pocket money, and I'll be handing it out in *small amounts* so that you can't spend it all on chocolate!" said Jess. "I highly recommend the squishy banana sweets, though."

When the tour was over, everyone gathered outside the hall. A CAMP BICKROSE banner was pinned above the door, with boards standing below that displayed the timetable for the next few days. Oralie gazed up at the banner, knitting her eyebrows together. "Camp Bickrose? I never knew it was called that," she said.

"Of course it is – Camp Bickrose, after Bickrose Hall!" said Yasmeen.

"What did you think it was called?" asked Rose.

Oralie put her face in her hands and mumbled, "You're going to think I'm really silly..."

"Go on, tell us," cajoled Amber.

Oralie looked up. "I thought it was Camp BigToes! I never saw it written down!"

Everyone laughed. Rose giggled until her stomach hurt. What had she been worrying about? She was going to love it here at Camp BigToes. She just had to stop thinking about Wriggly.